The Dress and the Girl

Words by
CAMILLE ANDROS

Pictures by
JULIE MORSTAD

Abrams Books for Young Readers

NEW YORK

For the Androutsos Family. Especially
Harry, who had the courage to start a new
life that made my life possible.
And to my mother, who made me many
beautiful dresses.
—C.A.

For Ida
—J.M.

Cataloging-in-Publication Data has been applied for and may
be obtained from the Library of Congress.

ISBN 978-1-4197-3161-7

Text copyright © 2018 Camille Andros
Illustrations copyright © 2018 Julie Morstad
Book design by Pamela Notarantonio

Printed and bound in China
10 9 8 7 6 5 4 3 2 1

Abrams Books for Young Readers are available at special discounts
when purchased in quantity for premiums and promotions as well
as fundraising or educational use. Special editions can also be created
to specification. For details, contact specialsales@abramsbooks.com
or the address below.

ABRAMS The Art of Books
195 Broadway, New York, NY 10007
abramsbooks.com

Back when time seemed slower
and life simpler, there was a dress.
A dress much like many others,
made for a girl by her mother.

The dress loved the girl,
and the girl loved the dress.

They spent each day together,
an ordinary girl wearing
an ordinary dress.

Every day the same story.

They rode in a wagon.

They sailed in a boat.

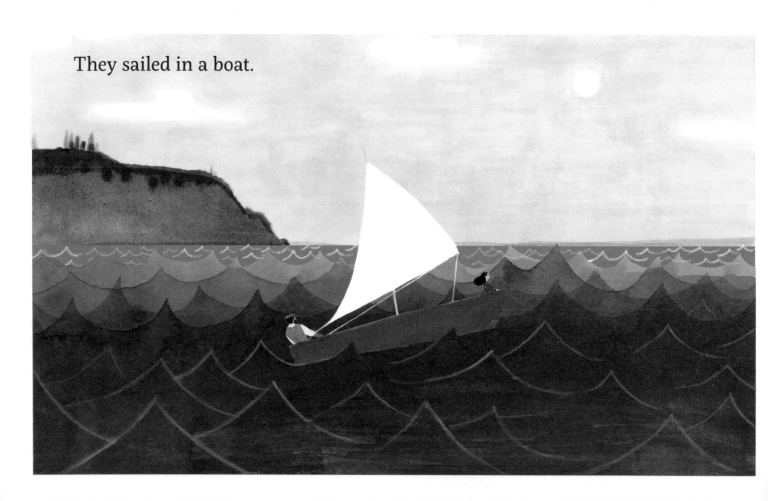

They went to school, jumped rope,

and played tag.

But they longed for the extraordinary.
Something singular, stunning, or sensational.

Instead, life continued on in quite an ordinary fashion.

Picking daffodils,

feeling the wind,

and staring at the stars.

Then one day, it came time to leave.

Their story was changing.

But still . . . they rode in a wagon.

They sailed in a boat.

They went to school, jumped rope,

and played tag.

Finally, the dress and the girl arrived.

They wondered if now was the time
for something singular, stunning,
or sensational.

For something extraordinary.

Instead, the dress was folded
up and placed into a trunk.

The dress waited for the girl to find her.

She waited and waited.

But the girl never came.

So, the dress set out to find the girl.

Alone, she rode in a wagon.

She sailed in a boat.

But she did not go to school, jump rope,

or play tag.

Instead, she traveled the world—searching.

Day after day,

week after week,

month after month,

and year after year.

Each day, week, month, and year telling a different story.

While she searched, the dress thought about the girl.
Feeling the wind dance with her was singular.
Picking daffodils together had been quite stunning.
And staring at the stars—sensational.
She missed the girl.

The dress was tired.
She needed to rest.

From her new spot, the dress could see the world all around her.
People moved quickly with heads down, passing by on their
way to important or not-so-important places.

One day, a woman walked by. She glanced up at the dress and stopped.
She did not move quickly down the street. She looked and looked.
In that look, the dress and the girl remembered.

They remembered riding in wagons.
They remembered sailing in boats.
They remembered going to school,
jumping rope, and playing tag.
They remembered daffodils,
dancing wind, and starry skies.

Every day its own story.
They had found each other at last.

And that was quite extraordinary.